MW00997930

Pet Shop Lullaby

Mary Ann Fraser

BOYDS MILLS
HONESDALE, PENNS

For Shannon Damon

Boyds Mills Press, Inc.
815 Church Street
Honesdale, Pennsylvania 18431
Printed in the United States of America

Library of Congress Cataloging-in-Publication Data

Fraser, Mary Ann.
Pet shop lullaby / Mary Ann Fraser. — 1st ed.
p. cm.
Summary: When the pet store closes for the night, a hamster's activities keep the other animals awake as they try to think of some way to put him to sleep.
ISBN 978-1-59078-618-5 (hardcover : alk. paper)
[1. Bedtime—Fiction. 2. Pets—Fiction.
3. Nocturnal animals—Fiction.] I. Title.
PZ7.F86455Pet 2009 [E]—dc22
2009019661

First edition
The text of this book is set in 30-point Optima.
The illustrations are done in acrylic.

10 9 8 7 6 5 4 3 2

Some animals sleep at night.

Some can't.

YAWN

Squeak

Squeak!
Squeak!

SQUEAK!

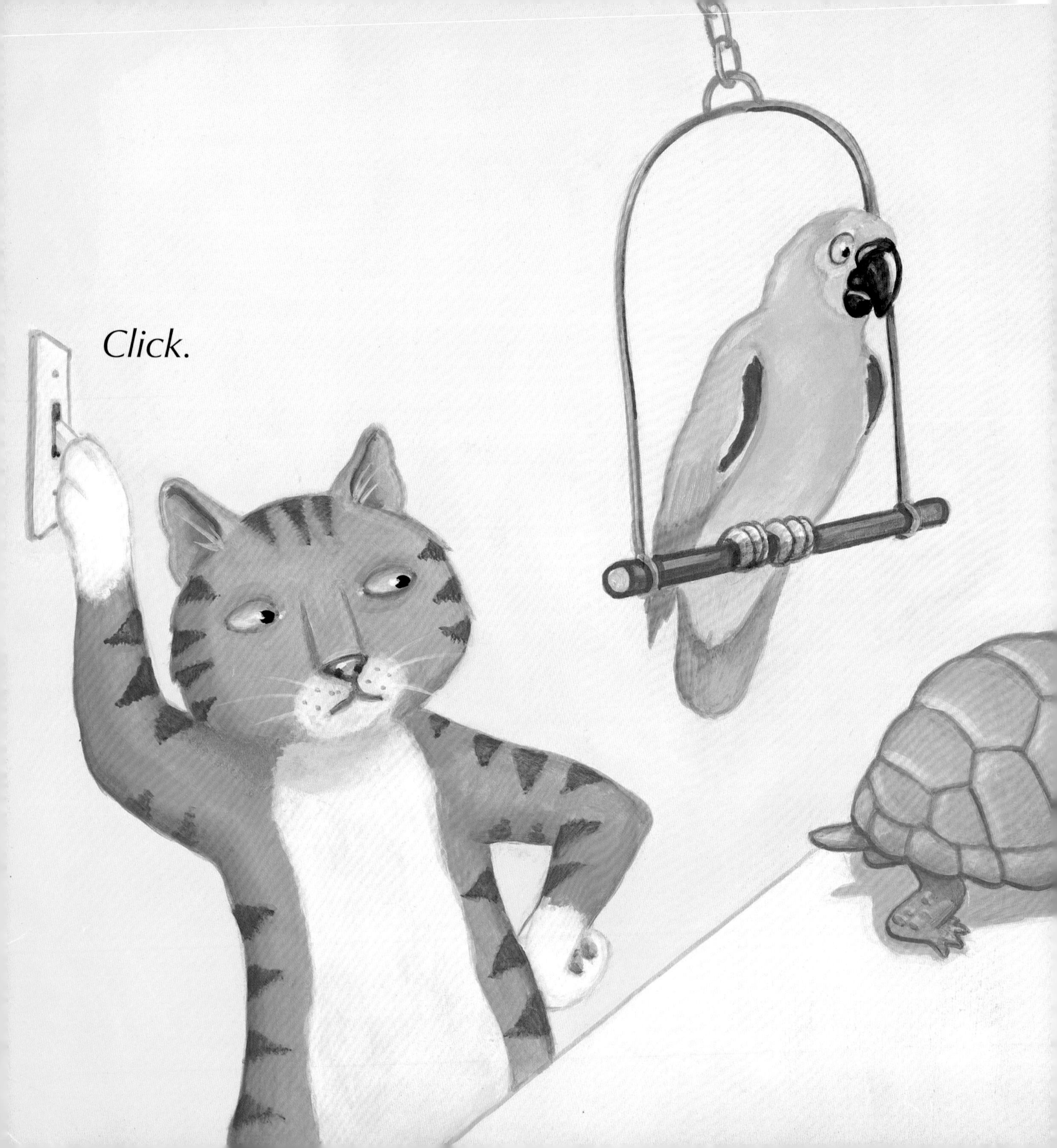

Click.

Sh-h-h-h-h
Click.

Scritch, scratch

Pitter-pat

Nibble, nibble, nibble,

munch munch

CRUNCH

Go to sleep!

How do you get a hamster to sleep?
Hypnosis?
Count kibble?
Bop him on the head?
Hmmm.

I know!

Give him a bath.

splish splash
BUDDY BATH

Brush his teeth.

Sing him a lullaby.

"R-r-r-rock-a-bye, baby,
on the treetop . . ."

Read him a story.

"Once upon a time there were three hamsters . . ."

Tuck him in.

Z-z-z-z-z-z-z-z-z-z

Z-Z-Z-Z-Z-Z

Z-Z-Z-Z-Z-Z

Ah-h-h-h-h

Sn-o-o-o-r-r-e

Z-Z-Z-Z-Z-Z-Z

w-e-e-e-o-o-h

Some animals sleep in the daytime.

Click.

Thump, thump, thump,

Meow-w-w

peep

Woof Woof

chirp

Squawk

And some wish they could.